Ge
of Au

Ann Pilling

Illustrated by Pauline Hazelwood

At their house, on the edge of Great Wood, the Baxter family were all very busy. Mum was up a ladder, cleaning the windows. Dad was inside, hoovering the carpets. In the garden, Jake and Sally were hoovering the dog. Aunt Mildred was coming on a visit.

The dog, whose name was Humphrey, didn't like being hoovered. It kept running off and rolling in the mud. "Come *here*, Humphrey!" yelled Jake. "You've got to look clean and tidy for Aunt Mildred."

Humphrey's ears drooped. He was a very little dog and he liked very little walks. Gentle trots round the garden suited him fine. He didn't like the long hikes he was forced to go on with Aunt Mildred. She was a fitness freak.

"Dad, why's Aunt Mildred coming?" asked Sally. It didn't seem five minutes since her last visit.

"Oh, you know …" he said vaguely, hoovering behind the bookcases (Aunt Mildred was bound to notice). But his face had a funny, far-away look. Sally went off to find her mother. She knew that look, it meant Bad News.

"Mum," she shouted up the ladder, "why's Aunt Mildred coming?"

"Oh, you know …" Mrs Baxter went on polishing the windows. She'd got the vague look too.

Sally went down the garden to find Jake. "Something's up," she told him, "and I think it's about Aunt Mildred." From the rhubarb patch, where he was rolling, Humphrey gave a little howl.

They didn't discover what the Bad News was till nearly tea-time. Then Jake found a newspaper with lists of houses for sale. One was called Cherry Cottage. It was small and thatched and it lay just the other side of Great Wood. Dad had put a red circle round it and written "Telephone Aunt Mildred" at the side.

Jake showed it to Sally. "It's much too small for us," she said, "You don't suppose …"

"I *do*," replied Jake. "She's always going on about moving to the country. This cottage looks perfect for her."

Sally felt faint. The thought of Aunt Mildred installed in Cherry Cottage for ever and ever was just too awful to think about. She'd never be away from their house, barging in and bossing, and interfering. "What are we going to *do*?" she whispered.

Jake shrugged. "Dunno." Then "Listen, perhaps Cherry Cottage is for a friend of hers, we can always hope …"

But when they asked Dad about the newspaper, all their hopes withered away. Aunt Mildred was *indeed* interested in buying Cherry Cottage, and she was coming to look at it this very weekend!

She was due at half-past six. Mum and Dad scurried round with dusters, Dad shoving piles of old magazines under the settee, Mum tidying baby Arthur's toys away into the washer. Aunt Mildred was a stickler for neatness and order.

Sally and Jake had to sit in the kitchen. They weren't allowed to watch TV in case they messed the best room up. Jake pushed a note under the door as they sat waiting for her to arrive. "We want our rights!" it said.

Then Sally sent another. "We demand to sit in the best room. We've missed 'Neighbours'." But Mum and Dad didn't seem to notice.

"I think they're a bit frightened of Aunt Mildred," said Jake.

Suddenly the doorbell rang loudly, three times. In his cot, baby Arthur wailed piteously. Humphrey dived under the grandfather clock. Clinging on to each other, like children about to enter a Ghost Train, Mum and Dad advanced towards the front door.

Dad was always saying that Aunt Mildred "wasn't such a bad old stick", but to Sally and Jake she was nothing *like* a stick. She was certainly tall, but she was very wide too; her arms were big and brawny, her legs like stout tree trunks. She had piercing blue eyes and her iron grey hair was set in big, hard waves, clamped on to her head like a sort of helmet.

The minute the front door was opened, she charged in. "Hello, everybody!" she boomed, putting down a large suitcase and an even larger cat basket.

She shook hands with Dad and she kissed Mum. Sally and Jake got hearty slaps on the back. "Hmm ..." she said, boring into them with her fierce blue eyes, "... these two are looking a bit peaky. Too much sitting around, I'd say, too much television. Oh well, we can soon sort that out. We've got all day tomorrow."

Sally and Jake looked at each other. Then they looked at Mum and Dad, but they'd got their vague faces on again. "It's a *plot*," Sally whispered. "I bet they're going off and leaving us with *her*."

Aunt Mildred didn't hear, she was too busy undoing the cat basket. She never came to stay without bringing Basil, her enormous tom-cat. The minute the lid was removed, he sprang out and tore off down the garden. "He adores the country," Aunt Mildred said. He'll just *love* Cherry Cottage. By the way, I'm moving in in three weeks. It's the perfect place for Basil and me."

At bedtime, they were permitted to sit in the best room for half an hour, with Aunt Mildred. She'd come to inspect Cherry Cottage, but also to "help out". Mum and

Dad were going on one of their book-buying expeditions. They had a shop in the town, not to sell new books but old ones, the mustier and the cobwebbier the better. Sometimes they went to special sales, to look for bargains. Sally and Jake found these book trips very boring. They were usually left in the car, to cope with Arthur.

"But Auntie's offered to look after you all tomorrow," Mum said. "Isn't that nice?"

"Great," Sally said flatly.

"Fantastic," said Jake, with a pained smile.

"So off you go to bed," Aunt Mildred ordered. "I'm coming myself in a minute. I need my beauty sleep."

Sally and Jake giggled as they went upstairs. *Beauty sleep.* Aunt Mildred looked more like a Sumo wrestler.

In the night she made terrific snoring noises. Then, early next morning, they were woken up by a heavy thumping. As it got louder, the whole house seemed to shake.

"She's doing her exercises," Jake whispered.

Stealthily they wriggled out of bed, stole along to Aunt Mildred's room and peeped in. All her windows were wide open. On the sill crouched Basil, hissing down into the garden, at Humphrey. Aunt Mildred, dressed in a shocking pink tracksuit, was running on the spot, her face bright red, her helmet of hair sticking up in tufts, like grey straw. "Come on, you two," she panted. "There's nothing like a bit of exercise, first thing in the morning."

"But we've not had any breakfast," protested Jake.

"And I didn't sleep very well," grumbled Sally.

"Oh rubbish! You're not made of china.
One, *Two*, One, *Two* ..." and suddenly they
were running too, and doing forward rolls,
and touching their toes, while Aunt Mildred
bellowed out instructions.

Then Arthur began to wail in his cot.

"Whoa!" she yelled. "That's enough for this morning. Let's get that baby sorted out."

"He likes Mum to see to him," gasped Sally.

"That'd be difficult. They left at the crack of dawn."

"*What*?" Sally and Jake said, in chorus.

"Oh yes, I told them to. No point in going to a book sale if you don't get first pick. Now, come along. Breakfast in ten minutes. Clean those teeth—and don't forget to wash behind your ears."

"How *could* they," spluttered Jake, as they went to the bathroom, "just go off, without *saying* anything, and leave us with her ..." He was furious.

Sally thought about it. "She bossed them into it," she said, "just like she forced us into the exercises. She's like an army tank. There's no arguing with her."

"Well, she's not bossing *me* around. If she doesn't stop —"

"Sally! Jake! BREAKFAST IS READY!" The voice that came up the stairs was definitely not to be ignored. Sheepishly, they slunk down to the kitchen and slid into their places.

Arthur, all clean and shining, was sitting in his high-chair waving a spoon. When he saw Sally, he started to grizzle, holding out his arms to be picked up.

"Now, *stoppit*, Arthur," Aunt Mildred said severely. "Eat your soldiers nicely, and don't make crumbs."

Arthur instantly stopped it, and began to cram eggy bread into his mouth.

"Don't *slouch*," she told Jake, giving him a poke in the back. "Shoulders down, chest up. Sally, chew your food before you swallow … Jake, use your napkin …" and so it went on, all through breakfast.

The two children felt murderous. Only little Arthur seemed happy. Big booming Aunt Mildred clearly fascinated him. As he stared at her, his button-bright eyes grew round with love.

The minute breakfast was over she told them to roll their sleeves up. "Everybody helps with washing up," she informed them, "and after that it's bedroom drill. I shall come upstairs and inspect in half an hour, and I expect everything to be clean and tidy. I'm not having your poor mother coming home to a messy house."

While they washed up, Aunt Mildred bore Arthur off to his room, to get him ready for the day. At the sink, Sally and Jake talked in whispers. They were hatching a plan. It was all very well behaving like a tank, Jake argued, but if people stood in its way then it had to stop.

"Aunt Mildred," Sally said sweetly when she came downstairs again, "we usually watch TV on Saturday, and Jake's got a computer. So if you don't mind, *dear* Aunt Mildred ..." and they sidled off down the hall.

"Games ... *computers* ... TELEVISION ..." The great voice followed them as they daringly flung open the door of the best room. "Oh no, I'm not having you lolling around this morning."

"But it's not 'lolling', Aunt Mildred. Jake's brilliant on his computer, and anyway, Mum always lets us watch Saturday TV."

"Not today. We're going for a nice long walk. Arthur's all ready. Aren't you, Arthur? Besides, you will find I have made arrangements for the television."

She had. It was covered in an old curtain, just like a parrot with its cage draped for the night. On top was a notice which said, "This device can seriously damage your health".

Jake and Sally stared at it in disbelief. "She's mad," whispered Jake. "We've got a mad woman looking after us."

"Mad Mildred," giggled Sally. If Aunt Mildred had heard, she was pretending not to.

"Come along," she said serenely, "bedroom drill in five minutes please, then I want you ready for the walk with your outdoor clothes on."

Open-mouthed, they watched her sail off to the kitchen with Arthur. She seemed bigger and squarer this morning, like a tank in fact. And she'd just rolled right over them.

The rest of the day was terrible. Only Arthur was happy, bobbing up and down in the baby-carrier which Aunt Mildred (with the straps fully extended) had slung on her back. Basil came with them, striding through the woods like a mini-lion, his fur all bushed up, his great whiskers quivering, hissing at everything in sight. Humphrey came too. Aunt Mildred made him. "He's far too fat," she'd told Sally and Jake. "A bit of exercise'll do him a power of good."

As they got deeper into the woods, he lagged further and further behind. "He's pathetic!" she shouted. "Look at Basil, he's miles ahead."

Sally and Jake didn't want to look at Basil. He was the most vicious, unfriendly, bad-tempered cat they'd ever met; quite a good companion for Mad Mildred. Poor old Humphrey was a much nicer pet. Sally

scooped him up tenderly, and carried him.
"Come on, Jake," she shouted, "race you to
the biggest log in the world," and they
disappeared into the bushes, to find their
favourite picnic place.

This was a clearing right in the middle of the wood where once, in a great storm, a huge tree had crashed down, making a bridge across the stream. They'd been walking for hours very fast, and they were looking forward to a rest now, to eating the picnic and to playing on the enormous log.

But Aunt Mildred had other plans. "*Right*," she said, checking her watch, "a ten-minute stop, then we'll have to get on," and she doled out packets of sandwiches. "Hurry up, there's a lot to do at home, before your parents get back."

Sally and Jake went off to sit on the log. They liked dangling their legs over the stream. But Aunt Mildred called them back. "You'll fall in," she shouted, "then it'll be colds all round." So instead, they crouched on the bank and looked round for some big stones to make a dam. "No messing about," she told them.

"You'll dirty your clothes." So Jake picked up a pebble, to do some skimming. "And no throwing stones," she warned him. "It's highly dangerous."

Miserably they chewed their fish-paste-and-lettuce sandwiches, staring longingly at the bubbling stream. Aunt Mildred chewed too, twenty times at least before swallowing. She seemed not to see the trees, just asking to be climbed, the water, just waiting to be paddled in. And Basil made such terrible hissing noises that all the birds flew away. Great Wood had never been so silent. It was the worst day out Sally and Jake could remember. They might as well have walked up and down a city street.

On the way back, it started raining. "Gee up, everybody," shouted Aunt Mildred, breaking into a trot. Arthur loved it, but Sally and Jake couldn't keep up. "Wait for *us*, Aunt Mildred," they hollered. "Can't we shelter somewhere till it stops? We're getting soaked."

But she only said, "Oh come *on*! You're not made of sugar," and ran even faster.

When they got home they were so
exhausted they just wanted to flop in front of
the TV. But the set was still covered up like a
parrot and anyway, Aunt Mildred had more
jobs lined up. Jake had to peel potatoes for
supper and Sally had to clean Mum's brass
candlesticks. She had sixteen pairs, all over the
house, and they were all very dirty. Only
Arthur was allowed to sleep, with his thumb
in his mouth and a little smile on his face. He
was obviously dreaming of Aunt Mildred.

"Can we have chips?" Jake asked timidly,
looking at his pan of potatoes.

"Certainly *not*," Aunt Mildred said crisply. "I've made a wholesome stew, much better for you than greasy chips."

So they ate bowls of watery stew with great lumps of turnip floating in it. Aunt Mildred had three lots. Sally and Jake took polite little mouthfuls. "It's like being in prison," Sally whispered. Jake didn't reply. He'd fallen asleep. Very soon, Sally found herself nodding too.

Aunt Mildred peered at them. "Oh dear," she said, "if you're as tired as that you'd better go and sit in the best room until your parents come home. Don't make nasty dents in the cushions though, and DON'T SWITCH ON THE TELEVISION."

They didn't. They just couldn't be bothered. All they wanted was to get away from Aunt Mildred. Side by side, in front of the shrouded TV set, they dozed peacefully.

"The house looks *wonderful*, Aunt Mildred," Mum was saying in rapture when they woke up, "and how kind of you to take the children for a walk. We had a marvellous day at the sale."

"Any time," purred Aunt Mildred. "If you'd like to go away again, just give me a ring. I'm quite used to children. Of course, it'll be so much easier when I'm living at Cherry Cottage."

"Mum," Jake said through gritted teeth, as he went up to bed, "if you *ever* leave us with Aunt Mildred again, I think I'll *kill* you!"

By the end of the summer, Aunt Mildred and Basil were installed in Cherry Cottage, but whenever they heard she was coming to visit, Sally and Jake made sure they had other things to do, friends to visit, or homework to finish. Sometimes they just hid in their room. They'd made such a fuss to Mum and Dad about the "day out" with Aunt Mildred that nothing was said about her looking after them again.

Then something awful happened. Grandad and Gran had a car accident. Grandad broke his arm and Gran broke three ribs. They felt very shaken and sore, and phoned to say how lovely it would be to see Mum and Dad.

The thing was that they lived in a very small house. It simply wouldn't fit all the Baxters.

Now that she was only just across Great Wood, said Grandad, could Aunt Mildred babysit perhaps, while Mum and Dad made a quick trip to see them?

Sally and Jake didn't even let their parents finish explaining. "We're *not* babies," they shouted, "and we don't want Aunt Mildred looking after us again. Last time was awful. We can stay here on our own, and we can look after Arthur ourselves."

"Don't be silly," Mum told them. "You're much too young."

"And anyway," said Dad, "it's only for one night. Think of poor Gran and Grandad. They've had a nasty shock."

But Sally and Jake could think only of Aunt Mildred. In the end, their parents made them a promise. She wouldn't come till after supper so there would be no danger of water-and-turnip stew. Arthur would already be tucked up in bed asleep, and they could sit in the best room and watch television. If they didn't want to talk to Aunt Mildred, they could go to bed early.

Grumbling and moaning, the two children finally said yes. They were fond of Gran and Grandad, otherwise they might have made more fuss. But as soon as they'd waved the car out of sight, Jake rolled his sleeves up, and became very business-like. "*Right*," he said. "Now they're out of the way, we can put my plan into action."

"What plan?" asked Sally.

Jake whispered in her ear. "You never know," he said, "Mad Mildred could have bugged the whole house. She could be listening to us, in Cherry Cottage."

For the next half hour they were both very busy, climbing up and down ladders, hunting around for papers and pencils, and being very nice to Arthur who was squalling in his cot. "*Do* go to sleep, Arthur. It's part of the plan," Sally pleaded. They got him quiet just in the nick of time. As his little squawks subsided, they saw Aunt Mildred marching up the garden path.

"She's here," hissed Jake to Sally. "Come *on* ..." and they crept downstairs.

At first there was silence, but not for very long. Soon they heard a ripping noise and saw Aunt Mildred peering in at the window. "What on earth does this mean, you silly children?" she yelled, waving the sheet of paper Sally had pinned on the front door. "POLITE NOTICE," it said. "AUNT MILDRED KEEP OUT. GUARD DOG ON PREMISES."

"Humph!" she grunted, when they didn't reply. "There's nothing polite about *this*. As for the dog, you can't be serious." (Humphrey, at the sound of her voice, had wriggled under the settee.) "Now, just let me in," she said. "I'm getting cold out here. It's raining. I think there's a storm brewing."

But Sally and Jake took no notice. So Aunt Mildred prowled round the house, trying all the windows. But Jake had made sure they were all securely fastened, and he'd nailed the loose ones up with a hammer. Fetching a step-ladder, Aunt Mildred climbed to the upper storey and tried all those windows too. Then she came down and rattled at the doors. But they were all carefully chained and bolted. "For the last time," she screeched through the letter-box, "OPEN THIS DOOR, OR YOU'LL BE SORRY!"

But Sally and Jake didn't answer.

At last, after more banging and rattling, she stormed off down the path and there was a delicious quiet, broken only by a whiney little wind that gusted through the letter-box. On the mat, Sally noticed a scrap of paper. "*In an emergency*," it said, in Aunt Mildred's writing, "ring 263301."

"Huh!" said Jake, screwing it up. "We don't need *that*. Come on," and they went off to the kitchen to make themselves some supper.

It was great, not having Aunt Mildred poking her nose in and interfering. On a tray, they put chocolate-spread sandwiches, peanuts, crisps and bottles of fizzy lemonade, and carried it into the best room. Then they put some music on the CD-player, the loud thumping kind that Aunt Mildred hated. They switched the electric fire on and lounged on the big settee, making dents in the cushions. When they'd finished all the food, they settled down to watch television. There was a spooky film on about a house full of vampires.

"*Great*!" said Jake, putting his feet on the coffee table. "If only Aunt Mildred could see us now."

The film had a lot of loud music, so loud it sometimes drowned out what the actors were saying. Then there was a sudden flash of light through the curtains and another, much louder noise. "Aunt Mildred was right," Sally said in a small voice. "There *is* a storm coming." She hated thunder.

"It'll blow over," Jake said, glued to the film. But it didn't. The blue flashes and the rumblings of the storm got closer and closer together. And it had suddenly become very hot. Sally pulled off her jumper and sat sweating in her T-shirt. Inside, she was starting to panic. If only Mum and Dad would come back.

There was a sudden spluttering noise from the television set and the picture turned into a series of dazzling white blobs. "Oh *no* ..." moaned Jake, "we were just getting to the best bit." He fiddled with the knobs, but then a notice appeared on the screen: DO NOT ADJUST YOUR SET. BREAK IN PROGRAMME IS DUE TO BAD WEATHER CONDITIONS. "That's that, then," he said, switching it off. "Now what are we going to do?" and he looked round rather moodily. Then Arthur started whimpering, up in his bedroom.

"It's the thunder," Sally whispered. "It must have woken him," and she ran upstairs to fetch him.

Nothing they could do would stop Arthur crying. They rocked him and they sang to him, they gave him a biscuit, some orange juice and his favourite toy rabbit. But the harder they tried, the louder he screamed. His face was deep scarlet, his mouth a great pink hole out of which the most hideous sounds were coming. When Sally tried to cuddle him he bunched up his tiny fists and pushed her away. "He's getting on my *nerves*," growled Jake. "Let's have some music."

But before he could put a CD on, Sally heard something, in between the thunder claps. "Listen," she said. When Arthur wasn't crying and the storm wasn't raging, they could hear a regular "plop-plopping" noise somewhere over their heads.

Jake was getting nervous too now. Sally could tell, because he hung on to her as they went up the stairs. The carpet was all wet and soggy and when they reached the landing they could see why. Water was dripping steadily through the ceiling, and there was a great bulge over their heads. "Don't touch it," said Jake "or the wallpaper'll burst and we'll get soaked."

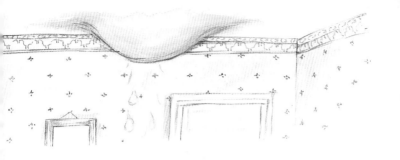

"But what on earth's *happening*?" Sally wanted to know.

"The gale must've blown some slates off the roof. Come on, there's no point in standing here." So they put a bucket under the drips and went back to the best room. Arthur was still crying. They put some pop music on, to try and distract him, but he only howled louder. "Perhaps the TV'll be OK now," Jake said hopefully, switching it on. "That might help." But the white blizzard on the screen was even thicker and outside the storm was raging harder than ever.

"I'm frightened," said Sally, trying her very best not to cry.

Suddenly, out in the garden, there was an almighty crash, a noise so massive it shook the house. Then all the lights went out. In terror Sally and Jake clung to one another, and to Arthur, as the orange bars of the electric fire turned paler and paler, finally disappearing into the blackness.

"Stay exactly where you are," said Jake. "I'll fetch the torch."

So Sally stood where the fire had been, clinging on to the howling baby, while Jake crashed about in the kitchen cupboards, looking for Dad's big flashlight. At last, Sally saw a wobbling ring of light coming towards her in the chilly dark, and she felt Jake's

fingers grip her arm. "Come on," he said, "there's nothing else for it. We're ringing 263301. Nobody lives round here, apart from Aunt Mildred."

Sally held the torch while he dialled the number. He waited and waited, but at last he thumped the receiver down. "It's no good," he said. "It's not ringing. The storm must have blown down the telephone cables."

Slowly, they crawled back towards the best room, crashing into the furniture, stubbing their toes, breaking things. At every fresh bang, Arthur wailed and screamed. Outside the gale raged on and the rain hurled itself against the windows. But Jake had brought anoraks from the hall cupboard, and a big rubber sheet to wrap the baby in. "Come on," he said, "if we can't ring Aunt Mildred, we'll just have to walk to Cherry Cottage. We can't stay here."

When they opened the front door, the wind nearly blew them flat. "I *can't*," wailed Sally, making even more noise than Arthur. "I'm too frightened …" and she turned back. But there was a sudden squelchy sound, then a kind of roar, and water started pouring down the stairs.

"It's the bulge," Jake shouted, "where the slates have been blown off. It must have burst. Come *on*, Sally."

Grabbing her hand, he shone the torch across the garden till they could see the little gate that led to Great Wood. Then they ran across the sodden grass with Humphrey at their heels. He had no intention of being left alone in that nasty, dark, cold house. Now they were on the move, Arthur seemed a bit happier too. He actually started to coo as he bobbed up and down in Sally's arms, his little pink head poking out of the rubber sheet.

Then Jake stopped dead, waving the torch.
Across the path that led to Cherry Cottage
was the most enormous tree trunk they had
ever seen, bigger even than "the biggest log in
the world". It was the four-hundred-year-old
oak that they could see from their bedroom
window. The great storm had brought it
crashing down.

In silence they stared at it, looking to the
left and to the right, into the endless trees. It

seemed to have no beginning and no end, and there was no way they could get round it, or over it, or through it. Humphrey gave a pathetic little jump and fell back helplessly, and Arthur started crying again.

"*Stoppit*, Arthur!" yelled Sally. In the hideous howling darkness, her voice echoed spookily, frightening her even more. "Just *stoppit*!" she screamed.

Then they heard a voice they knew. "Hello

... *Hello*! Is there anybody there?" A furry ginger lump suddenly flung itself over the tree and chased after Humphrey. "Aunt Mildred, it's Sally, Sally and Jake, and we've got Arthur. All the lights have gone off at home, and the electric fire, and there's water pouring down the stairs and ... HELP!"

"Now just stop snivelling, silly girl. Have you got a torch?"

"Yes," shouted Jake.

"Well, shine it on the log. I'm coming over."

But first there was a thump and something landed at their feet.

"Got the rope?"

"Yes," they shouted together, and they grabbed it.

"Now, fix the loop to one of the branches. And do it properly, mind. I hope you know your knots, Jake."

He didn't, but he tied it firmly to a thick
branch. Then he sat on it, just to make sure,
and cuddled Arthur in an attempt to stop him
howling.

"Now, I'm throwing something else over
first, and you've got to catch it. Ready?"
Across the enormous log sailed a carefully-
packed shopping basket with hot-water bottles
and thermos flasks poking out of the top. Sally
just managed to grab it and hung it on a
branch. Then she and Jake both stared into the
darkness.

The storm had dropped slightly and the wood was rustling mysteriously. But through the rustles, they could hear a heaving, grunting noise. The rope tightened, strained against the log and, far away, Aunt Mildred said, "*What* a good job I do my exercises every morning …"

Then a face appeared, all puffy and red, topped by a shiny yellow rain hat. Over she came, hauling herself up the rope, landed

neatly beside them and took the squalling Arthur in her arms. "Stoppit!" she said. He stopped instantly, and started sucking his thumb.

"*Right*," said Aunt Mildred. "Let's get going. Sally, you take my torch, and the basket. Jake, coil up the rope neatly, please, and watch where you're putting your feet, both of you. Your mother won't want muddy footprints all over her carpets." It was just as if she'd never been away.

The thermos flasks contained carrot soup, Aunt Mildred-style, but they were grateful for it. They'd got soaked to the skin out in Great Wood and their teeth were chattering with cold as they sat on the settee with their feet on the hot water bottles, while Aunt Mildred bustled around, mopping up water out in the hall. She brought all Mum's candlesticks into

the best room and arranged them along the
bookcases and cupboards. Then she lit the
candles. The flickering flames made darting
shadows everywhere. Arthur, dozing in
Sally's arms, chirruped happily at them and
fell asleep.

Now that there was enough light to see by,
Aunt Mildred brought wood and coal in from
the shed and lit a fire in the old hearth. "We
usually have the electric one on," Jake said, as
the kindling crackled and blazed up. "A
proper fire's great, though."

"Yes," said Aunt Mildred. "When I was a little girl, I used to sit by the fire with my mother, and she'd tell me stories."

Sally and Jake were silent, trying to picture this large, bossy woman with the iron hair as a child on her mother's lap. Somehow it wasn't as difficult as they'd expected. She'd looked young again, when she'd told them about sitting by the fire.

"We could read stories now," Sally said. "We can't watch TV," and she looked around for a book.

"I could *tell* you one," said Aunt Mildred.

"Once upon a time," she began, "there was this awful woman. She was very tall and rather fat and she had a niece and a nephew called Sally and Jake. In secret, they called her Mad Mildred ..."

Sally plucked at her cardigan. "Aunt Mildred—"

"Don't *interrupt*. As I say, she was really quite dreadful, you know, bossy and interfering. For instance, she dragged them off on walks and never let them have any fun, and she made them do housework on Saturday afternoons. Now one day ..."

"Aunt *Mildred*—" This time it was Jake.

"Don't—"

"We're sorry, Aunt Mildred," they said together and, in the candlelight, they both reached out and squeezed a plump, comforting hand.

There was silence. Then she squeezed back. She said, "I'm sorry too. Now, let's get on with the story. This terrible woman …"

As she unfolded the tale of the great storm, the screaming baby, the water pouring down the stairs, they got up from the fire-side rug and climbed on the cushions to sit beside her, snuggling up, while the wind howled round the house. It was funny, but she didn't seem like a tank any more, massive and square with nasty sharp corners. She was much more like the comfy old settee they were sitting on.